Joel Stewart

tiny cops

and

robbers

For Steve. J.S.

OXFORD
UNIVERSITY PRESS

Great Clarendon Street, Oxford OX2 6DP
Oxford University Press is a department of the University of Oxford.
It furthers the University's objective of excellence in research, scholarship,
and education by publishing worldwide. Oxford is a registered trade mark of
Oxford University Press in the UK and in certain other countries

Text and illustrations copyright © Joel Stewart 2016

The moral rights of the author and illustrator have been asserted
Database right Oxford University Press (maker)

First published 2016

Data available

ISBN: 978-0-19-274452-4 (paperback)
ISBN: 978-0-19-274453-1 (eBook)

1 3 5 7 9 10 8 6 4 2

Printed in China

Paper used in the production of this book is a natural,
recyclable product made from wood grown in sustainable forests.
The manufacturing process conforms to the environmental
regulations of the country of origin.

We're a happy family.

Mum, Dad, and Grandpa,
Baby Jack, and me, Big Ted!

There's just one problem.
    Tiny robbers in the house!

Ha ha!

They like to hide up on a high shelf,
with all the odds and ends.

What a bad lot, always looking for
something they can take.

But don't worry, here are our tiny coppers!

They've shined their boots and polished their badges. They're ready for anything.

Which is a good thing, because Robber Barry's off . . .

What's his dastardly plan?
He's tiptoeing closer to Daddy's toes . . .

The tiny coppers are on the case. Look at them go!

But Barry and Jim are quicker.
They're getting away!

step on it, Jim!

Oops! Beetle Jim's slipped up
and Barry's been flipped up.

Uh-oh!

Barry tumbles and turns

Ooh!

Err!

and PLONKS

right down beside the cops.

Humph!

Come with me, sonny!

Into the back of the van with you two.

Hooray for the tiny cops!

Now it's bath time for Baby Jack.

It's all lovely and bubbly and warm.

But uh-oh! I spy tiny robbers again.

It's Sly Sue and Stanley Mouse!
Watch out Mum, they've got
their eyes on your glasses!

Lovely
shiny loot!

Wheeeeeeeeeeeeee!

Too late, they've snatched them up
and now they're off!

But here's a light from the shadows.
It's two tiny coppers on patrol!

Eeek!

Sly Sue is dazzled.
Stanley Mouse is feeling dazed.

The cops have caught them
red-handed and rosy-cheeked.

Serves you right, tiny robbers.

Good job, tiny cops!

Peace at last.

Baby Jack is tucked up in bed
and Grandpa's taking a nap.

But wait, what's that
flippy-flapping sound?

Oh no! Here come Tim and
Tam on Robber Robin . . .

to grab Grandpa's wig!

Oh, the horror!
What an awful crime!

Copper Jane and Copper Kate
leap down with a hairnet.

Three more robbers for
the back of the van.

Nicely done, tiny cops!

Now our cops can celebrate!
What a great job they've done.

The house is safe once more.

Tiny cops!

Tiny cops!

Nobody stops the tiny cops!

Hang on, who's that
sneaking behind the fruit bowl?

Lovely
sneaky loot!

Disaster! The tiny cops forgot
this pair of sneaky sneaks!

It's Thieving Steve and
Burglar Worm and they've
nabbed the keys to the van!

Here we come, tiny robbers!

The tiny robbers are on the loose again!
What's their dreadful plot?

You can bet they're after something really
BIG this time . . .

JAIL

Let's go!

Free at last!

It's the crime of the century!
It's the worst of the lot!
Baby Jack can't lose his teddy.
Help me, tiny coppers, help!

Can PC Boots raise the alarm
in time?

But look out, tiny cops!

The tiny robbers won't give in
so easily . . .

Lovely snuggly!

Uh-oh!

Luckily, Copper Chris knows just what to do.

He bounces the robbers right off my tum . . .

ba doi oi

That's the way to do it, Ted!

oing!

and straight back into jail. Phew!

Hooray for the tiny cops!

Not again!

And me!

Back where I belong,
tucked up snug with Baby Jack.

Well done, tiny cops!
You've kept the peace for another day.

Goodnight, everyone.